CW00497422

PLAY BROADWAY

10 classic showstoppers for
FLUTE AND PIANO with ECD

Arranged by John Kember

FLUTE PART

The text paper used in this publication is a virgin fibre product that is manufactured in the UK to ISO 14001 standards. The wood fibre used is only sourced from managed forests using sustainable forestry principles. This paper is 100% recyclable.

To buy Faber Music publications or to find out about the full range of titles available please contact your local retailer or Faber Music sales enquiries:

Faber Music Limited, Burnt Mill, Elizabeth Way, Harlow CM20 2HX England
Tel: +44 (0) 1279 82 89 82   Fax: +44 (0) 1279 82 89 83
sales@fabermusic.com   fabermusic.com

Contents

Using the Enhanced CD (ECD)

A PDF of the piano accompaniment is included on the ECD for you to print out as necessary. A single print out of this musical work only is authorised. (This work includes copyright material owned by parties other than Faber Music, and unauthorised copies will constitute an infringement of the rights of such parties as well as those of Faber Music.) In order to view this file, you will need Adobe Reader, which is available for free download from www.adobe.com

© 2008 by Faber Music Ltd
First published in 2008 by Faber Music Ltd
Music processed by MusicSet 2000
Cover design by Kenosha
Printed in England by Caligraving Ltd
All rights reserved

ISBN10: 0-571-52631-4
EAN13: 978-0-571-52631-4

CD recorded in Zenith Studio, August 2007
Backings created and engineered by Jeff Hammer
Produced by Leigh Rumsey
℗ 2008 Faber Music Ltd © 2008 Faber Music Ltd

BACKING TRACK 1

Skimbleshanks: The Railway Cat

from *Cats*

Cats opened on Broadway in 1982 and is based on poems by T. S. Eliot from his *Old Possum's Book of Practical Cats*. Through song and dance, it describes a tribe of cats who gather once a year to choose who will make the journey to the Heaviside layer to be reborn. Skimbleshanks is a friendly uncle to all the cats and attends the trains he rides to make sure every detail is perfect.

Music by Andrew Lloyd Webber
Text by T. S. Eliot

Sixteen Going On Seventeen
from *The Sound of Music*

The Sound of Music opened on Broadway in 1959; the famous film version starring Julie Andrews was made in 1961. In Salzburg, Austria, a young woman studying to become a nun is sent to be governess to the seven children of a widowed naval commander. The children, initially hostile and mischievous, eventually come to love her when she introduces them to the joys of singing. In this song, the Captain's eldest daughter Leisl sings of her feelings on being 'Sixteen, going on seventeen'.

Lyrics by Oscar Hammerstein II
Music by Richard Rodgers

Not While I'm Around

from *Sweeney Todd*

Sweeney Todd opened on Broadway in 1979 and has since been widely performed in both theatres and opera houses. The setting is Mrs Lovett's Pie Shop in Victorian London, where young Tobias serves very dubious meat pies to the customers. Above the pie shop works Sweeney Todd – the 'demon barber of Fleet Street', bent on revenge against the judge for his wrongful arrest and deportation. Here Tobias sings protectively to Mrs Lovett 'No one's going to harm you, Not While I'm Around'.

Words and Music by Stephen Sondheim

BACKING TRACK [4]

Summer Nights
from *Grease*

Grease premiered in Chicago in 1971 as 'a play with music', but was then reworked as a musical and appeared on Broadway in 1972. However, it became most popular through the 1978 film starring Olivia Newton-John and John Travolta. Set in the summer of 1959, it tells the story of Danny Zuko, member of boy gang the T-Birds, and Sandy, an innocent girl from Australia. This opening song takes place on the first day of a new school year as Danny tells his friends about his summer romance.

Words and Music by Jim Jacobs and Warren Casey

sub. *p* $\boldsymbol{f}$

mf

Poco meno mosso

mf

meno mosso

$\boldsymbol{f}$

rit. gliss.

mp $\boldsymbol{f}$

8

BACKING TRACK 5

Mister Cellophane
from *Chicago*

The show billed as 'murderous, seductive and All That Jazz' has been a hit since its original production in 1975, but really became a major hit on Broadway in 1996. The action takes place in Chicago in the 1920s and revolves around a vaudeville double act. The 'Mister Cellophane' of this song is Amos Hart, the husband who never seems to get noticed! 'Mister Cellophane, 'cause you look right through me, Walk right by me, And never know I'm there'.

Words by Fred Ebb
Music by John Kander

© 1975 (renewed) Unichappell Music Inc and Kander & Ebb Inc, USA
Warner/Chappell North America Ltd, London W6 8BS

Anything Goes
from *Anything Goes*

Anything Goes opened in New York in 1934 and became the fourth longest-running musical of the 1930s. The action takes place aboard the S.S. America, sailing from New York to England. On board are an odd assortment of passengers including a gangster, a wealthy mother and daughter, a nightclub singer, and a New York businessman.

Words and Music by Cole Porter

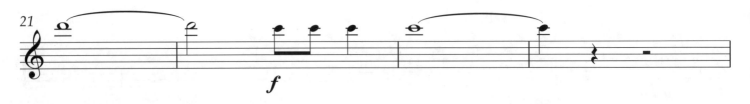

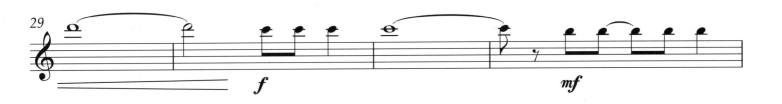

BACKING TRACK 7

Can You Feel The Love Tonight?

from *The Lion King*

Originally a film made by Disney Studios in 1994, the musical version of *The Lion King* moved to the Broadway stage in 1997. The show features actors in animal costumes and giant puppets who tell the story of a young lion in Africa named Simba, who learns of his place in the 'Circle of Life' while struggling through various obstacles to become the rightful king.

Music by Elton John
Words by Tim Rice

Chim Chim Cher-ee
from *Mary Poppins*

The 1964 film, now a West End and Broadway stage musical, starred Julie Andrews in the title role and Dick Van Dyke as the ever-present 'Jack-of-all-trades'. Based on the children's books by P. L Travers, Mary Poppins is an unconventional nanny who comes to live with the well-to-do Banks family in London and sets about putting the family to rights – with lots of madcap adventures along the way. In this scene they explore the world of the chimney sweeps above London.

Words and Music by Richard Sherman and Robert Sherman

Wouldn't It Be Loverly
from *My Fair Lady*

My Fair Lady is based on George Bernard Shaw's *Pygmalion*, and opened on Broadway in 1956. The production starred Julie Andrews as Eliza Doolittle and Rex Harrison as the professor, Henry Higgins. In this song, Eliza (a cockney flower girl in London's Covent Garden) dreams of setting up her own flower shop. 'All I want is a room somewhere, Far away from the cold night air. With one enormous chair, Oh, wouldn't it be loverly?'

Words by Alan Jay Lerner
Music by Frederick Loewe

Embraceable You
from *Girl Crazy*

Girl Crazy opened at the Alvin Theatre on Broadway in 1930. It ran for 272 performances and made stars of both Ginger Rogers and Ethel Merman. The pit orchestra also contained four musical legends: Glenn Miller, Gene Krupa, Tommy Dorsey and Benny Goodman. It was re-staged on Broadway in 1992 under the new title of *Crazy For You*. The song 'I Got Rhythm' also comes from the original 1930 show.

Music and Lyrics by George Gershwin and Ira Gershwin

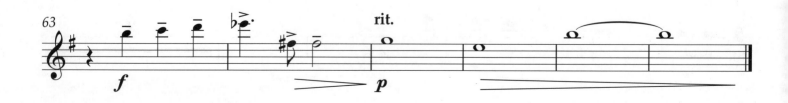